PADDINGTON AT THE TOWER

Paddington Picture Book 6

For older children Michael Bond has written
ten Paddington story books, all illustrated
by Peggy Fortnum

Text © Michael Bond 1975
Illustrations © Fred Banbery and
William Collins Sons & Co Ltd 1975

First published 1975

ISBN 0 00 182132 6

Made and Printed in Great Britain by
William Collins Sons & Co Ltd Glasgow

Paddington
at the Tower

MICHAEL BOND
illustrated by
FRED BANBERY

COLLINS
ST JAMES'S PLACE, LONDON

Soon after Paddington went to live at number
thirty-two Windsor Gardens Mr and Mrs Brown
gave him a basket on wheels.

The Browns' house was near the Portobello Road,

where there was a large market, and every
morning Paddington went there to do his shopping.

After calling at the baker's, where he had a
standing order for buns, he then went on to see
his friend Mr Gruber, who kept an antique shop.

Paddington liked Mr Gruber's shop. It was so full of things it was like Aladdin's cave.

Every day Mr Gruber made some cocoa and they had their "elevenses" together.

One morning, however, Paddington had a
surprise. When he reached the shop he found Mr
Gruber busy putting up his shutters.

"It's Easter Monday, Mr Brown," he said.

"And as it's such a nice day I thought I would take

you and Jonathan and Judy on a mystery outing."
Paddington was very excited. He hurried back
home to tell the others and then he began making
some marmalade sandwiches. He soon had so
many he could hardly close the lid of his suitcase.

Later that morning they set off, and Mr Gruber
found them a seat right at the front of the bus so
that he could point out the interesting sights on
the way.

They had been travelling for quite a while

when Jonathan and Judy suddenly let out a cry.

"I know where we're going," said Judy, as they turned a corner.

"It's the Tower of London!" exclaimed Jonathan.

Paddington had never been to the Tower of London before and he was most impressed. It was much, much bigger than he had pictured. As they reached the entrance a man in a

strange uniform stepped forward to take their
tickets.

"That's one of the Beefeaters," whispered
Jonathan. "They look after the Tower."

"They're really Yeomen Warders," explained
Judy. "But they get called Beefeaters because in
the old days they used to taste all the Royal food
to make sure it was safe to eat."

Paddington raised his hat politely and then
opened his suitcase.

"Would you like one of my marmalade
sandwiches?" he asked. "I expect it will make a
nice change from beef."

"A *marmalade sandwich*!" spluttered the
Beefeater. He held the object up between his
thumb and forefinger and stared at it as if he
could hardly believe his eyes.

But when he looked down again Paddington
had gone.

Taking one look at the expression on the man's
face, he picked up his suitcase and hurried after
the others. Several more sandwiches dropped out
on the way, but by then he was much too upset
to notice.

Mr Gruber hastily led them through an arch.
When they were safely round the corner he
stopped beside a large cage.

"This is where they keep the ravens, Mr
Brown," he said.

"They've always had ravens here and it's said
that if they ever fly away, then the Tower will
fall down."

Paddington peered at the empty cage. "Perhaps
we'd better go soon, Mr Gruber," he said anxiously.

Mr Gruber laughed. "I don't think there's any
fear of it happening just yet, Mr Brown," he said.
"That Tower looks very solid to me."

He pointed towards a large black bird standing
watching them. "Besides, there's at least one
raven keeping an eye on things."

"He looks as if he's got his eye on Paddington,"
said Judy.

Next, Mr Gruber took them to a room deep
under the ground.

"This is where the Crown Jewels are kept,"
whispered Judy. "They are made of gold and
they are very valuable. That's why they are kept
behind glass."

Mr Gruber showed them
the St Edward's Crown

. . . the Orb and Sceptre

. . . and an Ampula
and Spoon for holy oil.

"They were all used by the Queen at her
Coronation," he explained. "The crown has over
four hundred precious stones and it weighs
nearly five pounds!"

Paddington's eyes grew larger and larger. He
could quite see why no-one wanted the Tower to
fall down.

When they came out of the Jewel House
Paddington noticed a strange thing. There were
now two ravens watching him.

A moment later two more arrived, and all four
stared at him as he went past.

Paddington gave them a hard stare back, but for once it didn't seem to have any effect.

"Perhaps we'd better have our picnic outside by the river," said Judy, when she saw the worried look on Paddington's face. "They won't follow you out there."

But the ravens did follow Paddington, and by
the time they reached the gate there were so
many he'd nearly lost count.

"And where do you think you are going with our ravens, young fellow-me-bear?" asked the Beefeater in charge.

"*He's* not going anywhere with them," said Jonathan and Judy. "*They're* going with him."

"It makes no difference," said the man sternly. "I'm not letting them leave here and risk having the place fall down. That bear will **have to** stay in the Tower until we've decided **what's best**."

"Oh, crikey!" groaned Jonathan. "Fancy Paddington being sent to the Tower."

Suddenly Mr Gruber had an idea. "You know what?" he said excitedly. "I don't think it's Mr Brown they're after at all. I think it's his sandwiches!"

Paddington gazed at Mr Gruber in astonishment. "My sandwiches!" he exclaimed hotly.

But Mr Gruber was right. Sure enough, as
soon as Paddington opened his suitcase all the
ravens gathered round and began pecking at the
contents.

"All the years I've been here," said the Beefeater,
"and I never knew ravens like marmalade."
    He looked at Paddington with new respect.
"Perhaps you could give me your address, sir.

Then if any of our birds ever get lost we can
send for you.

"We may even be able to find you a special
jar of marmalade to keep by you in case it's
needed in a hurry."

"Trust Paddington to get sent to the Tower and then end up with a jar of marmalade!" exclaimed Judy.

Paddington looked at it happily. "If I'm to be a Marmalade-eater," he announced, "perhaps I'd better test it now – just to make sure!"